For all those who have devoted their lives
to putting others first.
To my family, friends and my three reasons
for being, thank you for all you are and do.
Always beside you!

Published in the United Kingdom by:

Blue Falcon Publishing
The Mill, Pury Hill Business Park,
Alderton Road, Towcester
Northamptonshire NN12 7LS
Email: books@bluefalconpublishing.co.uk
Web: www.bluefalconpublishing.co.uk

Copyright © Brendan Bolger, 2022
Illustrated by Leah Rowe

A CIP record of this book is available from the British Library.

First printed March 2022
ISBN 9781912765461

Trouble
On Farmer Tigg's Farm

Written by Brendan Bolger

Illustrated by Leah Rowe

Our story begins not so long ago,
On a very small farm, 10 acres or so.
There lived Farmer Tigg and his very small crew,
Four cows, five sheep and a duckling or two.
A horse named Rosie, a llama named Dave,
Dylan the dog, who just couldn't behave.

Alexander the bull, and Molly the cat,
On Farmer Tigg's lap she would always be sat.
Colin the rooster, who was kind and clever,
Percy the peacock and one goose named Trevor.
They all lived together, content as can be,
Healthy and playful as they all roamed free.

An ordinary farm, I hear you all cry,
But this one's not ordinary, and I'll tell you why!
For all of these creatures are rather unique,
They don't baa or moo – they can actually speak!
Yes, they talk and they chatter just like you and me,
And instead of water they'd rather drink tea.
They wear shoes and socks, as well as old clothes.
Why, you may ask. Well, nobody knows!

They lived happily on this most friendly farm,
For Farmer Tigg would let them come to no harm.
He taught them to cook, read and always play fair,
And how to stay safe when he wouldn't be there.
And good job he did, because you never know,
When someone might call, be they friend or a foe.
And that's just what happened one bright summer's morn,
While the farmer was busy harvesting corn.

Nigel the croc who'd escaped from the zoo,
Arrived at the farm to cause a to-do.
Now, Nigel was nasty, in fact he was vile,
But what else would you expect, he's a croc from the Nile?

With powerful jaws and a great sense of smell,
And sharp jagged teeth that his victims knew well.
Oh Nigel was frightful, of that there's no doubt,
As our farmyard friends were about to find out!

He walked through a gate just as calm as could be,
Trying to decide what he'd have for his tea.
Will it be duck, lamb or possibly beef?
He thought to himself as he licked his sharp teeth.
"All of them, of course!" he declared with a laugh.
"It'll make a nice change. I'm sick of giraffe."

THANK YOU FOR
ANY OLD CLOTHES

He prowled through the farm, his eyes searching around,
But not one farmyard creature was there to be found.
"Where are they?" he grumbled. "Oh, where can they be?
There's no point in running or hiding from me.
I'm Nigel I am, I'm the king of the Nile,
And I'm coming to get you!" he snarled with a smile.

He walked, and he stalked, then suddenly stopped still,
When he noticed a building on top of a hill.

"Oi Oi!" exclaimed Nigel. "What do we have here?
It looks like a hay barn," he said with a sneer.

"Now if I'm correct, and I usually am,
That's where I'll find my duck, beef and lamb!"

Oi Oi !

"Onwards!" he bellowed,
the horrible beast,
And onwards he went
as he dreamt of his feast.

He thought of the creatures on which he would dine,
A glorious menu he couldn't decline.
"Yummy!" he thought, as he crept like a thief,
Wiping drool from his mouth with an old handkerchief.

One step, then two steps, then twenty steps more,
And the ghastly old croc had arrived at the door.
"At long last," he thought. "Let the banquet begin!"
But there was just one problem... he couldn't get in!
With a rumbling tummy he could take no more,
And bursting with anger he crashed through the door.

CRAASSSHHH!

Perhaps you can picture the creatures' surprise,
At the curious sight that now greeted their eyes.
But the animals didn't stir, no, not a jot,
Because these ones are special, or had you forgot?

They looked at the croc and the mess he'd just made.
They noticed his teeth, but they still weren't afraid.
"Hello there!" crowed Colin, "Cocka-how-do-you-do?
There's a door 'round the corner you could have walked through."

"Never mind that!" angry Nigel snarled back,
As he crept towards Colin, still perched on a sack.
"Good day, my dear fellow, how can I help you?"
Asked Colin politely, whilst sipping his brew.
"A good day it is, a great day indeed!"
replied nasty Nigel preparing to feed.
"I'm Nigel the croc, the king of the Nile,
And sadly for you, I haven't dined for a while.

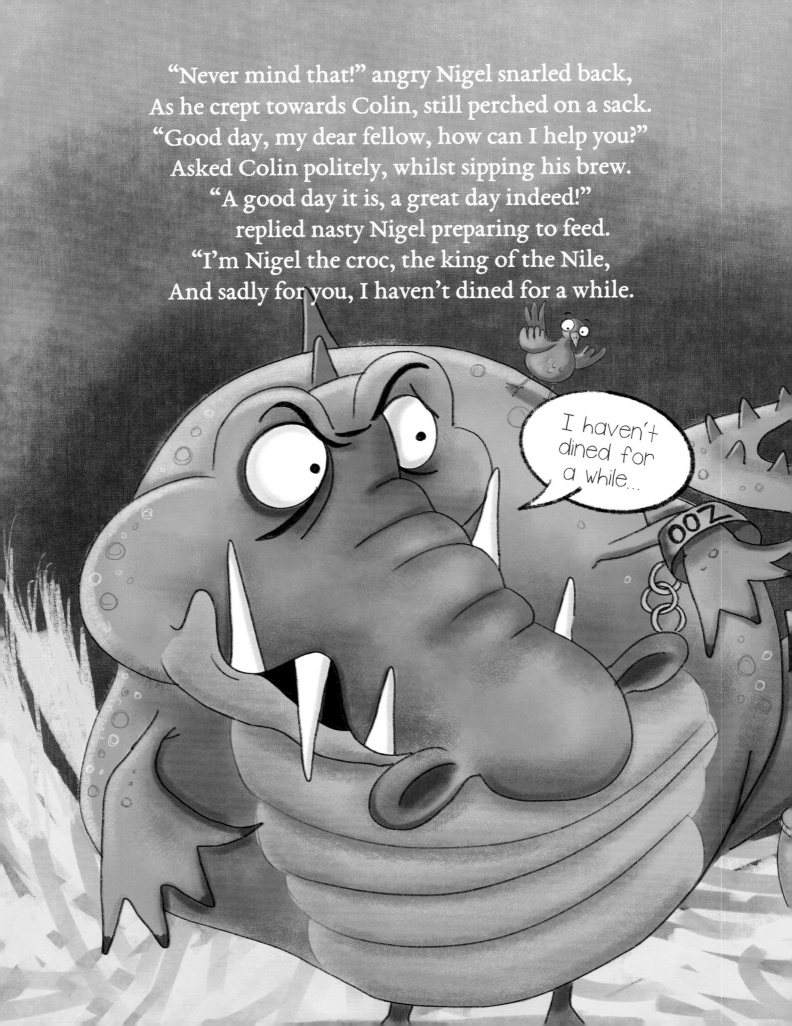

"Now, that makes me hungry, and angry and mean
And on juicy chicken I'm ever so keen!"
"Chicken – that's fowl!" wily Colin declared,
recalling the plan that the animals shared.
"Try this instead," our feathered friend said,
As he pulled from a basket two slices of bread.
In between them was pickle and strong cheddar cheese,
Cut in perfect triangles, certain to please.

"What's this?" Nigel asked with a look of surprise.
"I've never 'ad food that ain't covered in flies!"
"Well, try them, good man, and soon you will see,
They're far, far tastier and less bony than me!"

"I'll 'ave 'em," Nige said, "but they'd better be great,
Or you'll be the one to end up on my plate."
He scoffed downed the sandwiches, pickle and all,
And looked at the rooster who'd had a close call.
"Tasty, but not filling!" he said to his prey,
Then he stood and turned tail, then swaggered away.

But he didn't go far. No, not far at all,
Just a few little strides to the billy goats' stall.

The kids and old Billy were playing in hay,
And paused for a second as Nige came their way,
But then they continued for they knew the plan,
As Betty Goat offered a strawberry flan.
"Do have some," she said, "please, don't be shy,
Or if you'd prefer it we've got apple pie.

"With rich creamy custard and cherries on top.
Homemade, I assure you, not bought in a shop!"
Well, try it he did, and he scoffed the lot down.
"Is that all you've got?" he snapped with a frown.

"Of course not," smiled Betty, "we've got so much more!"
As she trotted her way to the pantry door.
"Help yourself, deary, please eat all you wish.
You must try the sushi, it's simply delish!"

In Nigel went, the greedy old croc,
Eating crackers and crumpets and cheese by the block.
Spring rolls, samosas, and warm, buttered toast,
But 'twas Yorkshires and gravy that he liked the most!

"Now time for dessert," Nigel thought to himself,
Eyeing the trifles upon the top shelf.
One trifle, two trifles, three trifles more,
Then juicy fruit salad and ice cream galore!
He gobbled and guzzled until he was stuffed,
Then he leaned back and belched loudly, "I've 'ad enough!"

Beaming with pleasure, Nigel sauntered out,
With custard and chocolate all over his snout.
"Now that was fantastic, I simply must say,"
As he made himself comfy on a big pile of hay.
"If it's okay with you, I'll 'ave a quick nap –
Bring me a pillow, will you, my old chap?"
"Try these," said Trevor, and gave the croc two.
"I made them this week, so they're practically new."

Off Nigel dozed, content and well fed,
Snoring with happiness in his hay bed.

When Nigel woke up from his quick four-hour snooze,
He looked round the barn at the horse, goats and ewes,
Who were playing and baking and crafting once more,
While Alexander was busy fixing the door.
"Hmmm!" he considered. "I could live like this.
The boring zoo meals I really won't miss."

But then he had feelings he'd not felt before,
Feelings so strong that he couldn't ignore,
Of guilt and of shame, for the things he had done.
He had to say something. "Er... hello, everyone!"
They stopped and stood still and looked over his way,
Waiting to hear what the croc had to say.

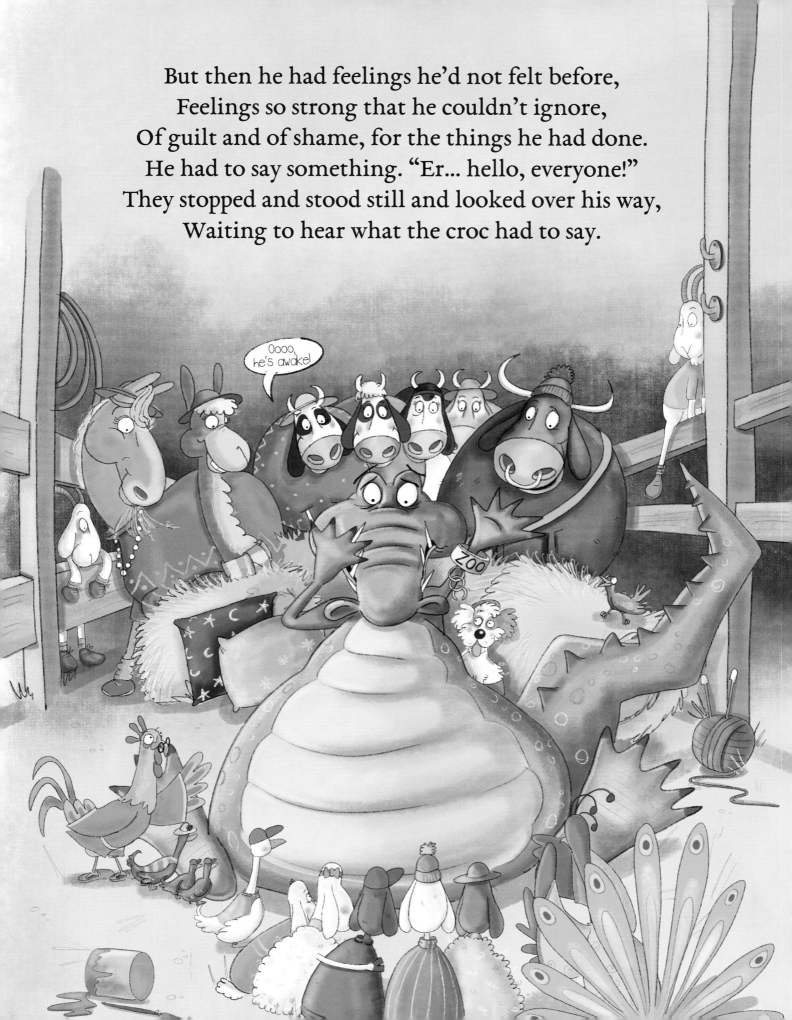

"I'm sorry," Nige sobbed, "for causing such harm.
I didn't realise it was this type of farm,
Where you are all helpful and care for each other.
Although not the same, you're like sister and brother.
A farm full of happiness, where everyone's kind,
Places like this are not easy to find.

"And if you will have me, I'd love to stay here."
To which all the animals let out a great cheer!
"Of course you can stay!" his friends all replied,
Making Nigel feel fuzzy and warm deep inside.

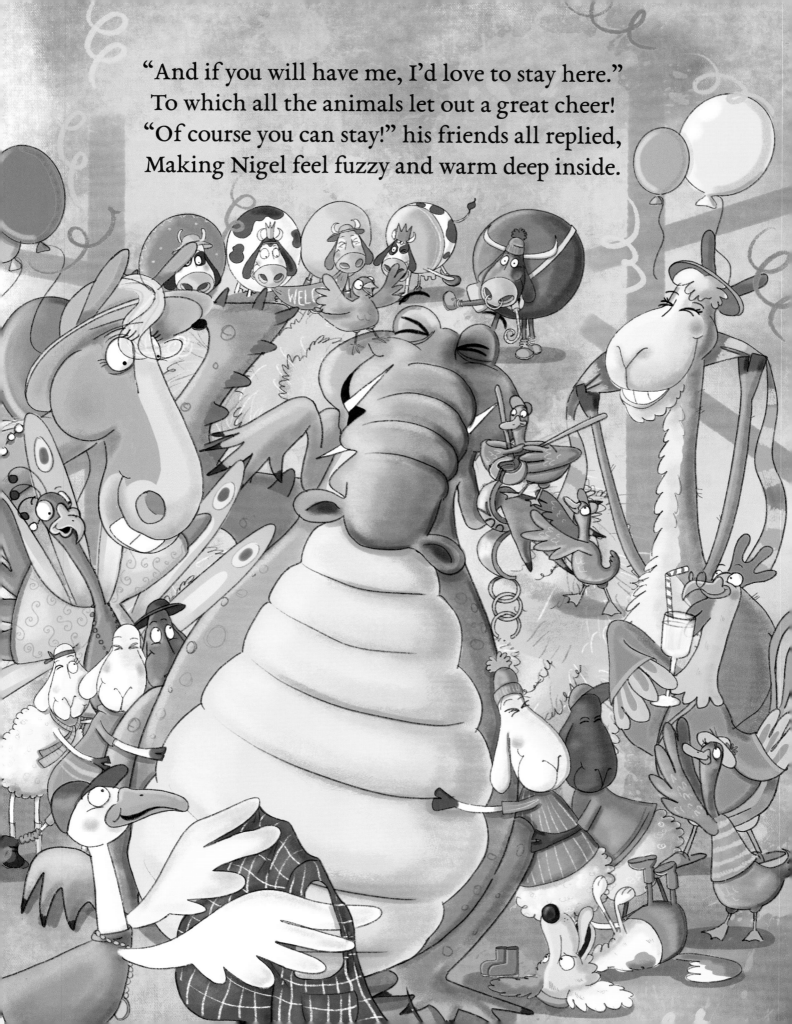

"We knew that you would, it only makes sense,"
Whinnied Rosie the horse from over her fence.
"So while you were napping we added a pool.
We know how important it is to stay cool."
"Goodness," said Nige, "what a special surprise!"
Wiping a tear or two from his eyes.

"It's settled," crowed Colin. "Cock-a-doodle-do!
You're part of our family, part of our crew."
Now they all live together, content as can be,
Healthy and playful and all roaming free.

Supporting Charity

Through the work of Cúram Le Chéile Ltd. 100% of net profits from the sale of this book will be donated to the following charities and organisations:

Children's Health Foundation (Dublin - Ireland) - 10%
Cancer Funds for Children (Down and Mayo, Ireland) - 10%
Amber Women's Refuge (Kilkenny, Ireland) - 10%
Solas Cancer Support Centre (Waterford, Ireland) - 10%
My Canine Companion (Cork, Ireland) - 10%
Great Ormond Street Hospital (London, UK) via Work for Good - 10%
Care for Wild Rhino Sanctuary (South Africa) - 25%
The Beehive Foundation (Kenya) - 5%
EPIC Arts (Cambodia) - 5%
The One Tree Planted Organization - 5%

For more information on our fundraising initiatives and the charities we are supporting please visit www.curamlecheile.com.